# The Clumsies

## make a mess of the Airport

First published in paperback in Great Britain by
HarperCollins *Children's Books* in 2012
HarperCollins *Children's Books* is a division of HarperCollins*Publishers* Ltd
1 London Bridge Street, London SE1 9GF
Visit us on the web at www.harpercollins.co.uk

Text copyright © Sorrel Anderson 2012

Illustrations copyright © Nicola Slater 2012

ISBN: 978-0-00-743869-3

Printed by CPI Group (UK) Ltd, Croydon CR0 4YY

# The Clumsies

## make a mess of the Airport

BY SORREL ANDERSON

HarperCollins *Children's Books*

Illustrated by nicola Slater

**The Clumsies** also make a mess in:

# Contents

For R. J. P and D. M. P

# Check in, check out, shake it all about

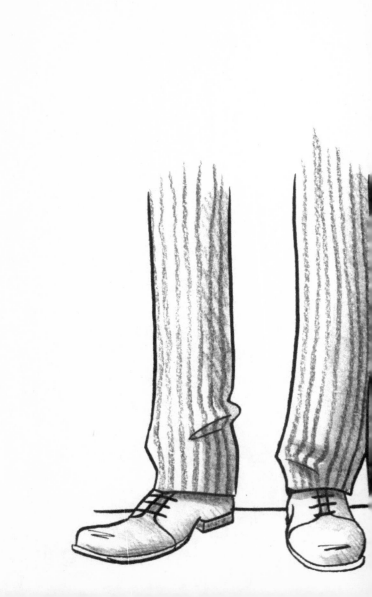

It was a Tuesday morning and Howard and the Clumsies were going on holiday. Howard was carrying a **large** bag and feeling tense. Purvis was carrying a **small** bag and feeling eager.

Mickey Thompson was carrying
a sombrero and staring at
a vending machine while
Allen the dog and Ortrud the
elephant (carrying nothing),
were looking a little bit
nervous as they gazed around
the airport's vast departure hall.

Howard glanced down at them.

'There's no need for *nerves*,' he said, bracingly. 'We're all going to have a nice, relaxing time, aren't we?'

Allen and Ortrud nodded *nervously*, Purvis nodded eagerly and Mickey Thompson began to b o u n c e.

'We're going to FLY!'
he **shouted**.

'Yes, indeed,' said Howard.
'Our holiday starts right here;
the travelling's all part of the
fun.'

'Oh, I can't wait, I
can't wait,' said Mickey
Thompson. He stuck out his
arms like wings and raced off
**shouting**, 'WHeeeeeeeeeeeeeeeeeeeeeeeeeeeeeeee!'

'COME BACK,'
*yelled* Howard.

'wheeeeeeeeeeeeeeeeeeeeeeee!'

went Mickey Thompson,
racing back and **bashing** into
Howard's foot.

'Ouch,'

said Howard.

'Sorry, Howard,' said Purvis, grabbing his brother before he could set off again. 'He's over-excited about the flying.'

'We're going to fly a million miles fast and a billion miles **higher** than the sun,' announced Mickey Thompson. Ortrud **trumpeted** in alarm and Allen looked a little faint.

'PURVIS!' said Howard, **loudly**. 'Tell us which part of the holiday *you're* most looking forward to.'

'Travelling wisely,' said Purvis, delving into his bag and producing a well-thumbed book called "*The Wise Traveller*".

'It has all sorts of useful information,' he said, 'but there were one or two things I wanted to ask you, Howard.'

'Ask away,' said Howard. Purvis opened the book and out fluttered a drawing of Howard in a flowery swimsuit, lying on a tropical-looking beach.

'Hang
o
n
a minute,'

said Howard.

'Yes, Hang
o
n
a minute,'

said Mickey Thompson. 'That's
my drawing; I did it last week.'

'I know,' said Purvis.
'I borrowed it to use as a
bookmark.'

'I've been looking for it
everywhere,' grumbled

17

Mickey Thompson. 'I wanted to

STICK it up in the office.'

'We will,' said Purvis, 'as soon as we get back from holiday.'

'Oh no we won't,' said Howard. 'It's unflattering.'

'It isn't,' protested Mickey Thompson. 'It looks just like you.'

'I disagree,' said Howard.

'I think it's rather good,' said Purvis.

'So do I,' said Mickey Thompson.

'But, but,' *spluttered* Howard.

'Listen,' said Purvis, tapping his book.

'"The wise traveller is a calm traveller, remaining cheerful at all times and never bickering with his, or her, companions."'

'Sensible advice,' Sighed Howard. 'Now, what was it you wanted to ask?'

'**Well**,' said Purvis,
'there are chapters on safaris
and camel trains and hot air
ballooning, and what to wear

and what to pack and what to
say, but I couldn't find anything
about airports.'

'Nothing at all?' said Howard, sounding *surprised*.

'No,' said Purvis, 'so I don't know what it is we're supposed to do here.'

'It's simple,' said Howard. 'First we check in at **"check in"**. He pointed at a sign marked **"Check in"**, and everyone looked and nodded.

**'Check in,'** muttered Mickey Thompson. **'Check in.'**

**Security**

'Then we go through security.' Howard pointed at a **long** queue of people shuffling quietly under a sign marked **"Security"**. Everyone nodded and looked.

'After security we leave the **"landside"** part of the airport, which is here, and go to the **"airside"**

**Airside**

part of the airport, which is through there.' Howard pointed at some double doors marked **"Airside through here"**, and everyone looked slightly CONFUSED.

'Then we wait until it's time for us to fly.'

Mickey Thompson started bouncing again and stuck out his arms.

'Not so *fast*,' said Howard, grabbing him before he could run off. 'This airport is a **large** and busy place full of **large** and busy people, so it's very important we all keep together: we don't want anyone getting lost, or **SQUASHED**, do we?'

'No, Howard,' said the mice.

'No, Howard,' agreed Howard. 'Please explain it to Allen and Ortrud, too.'

'They heard you,' said Purvis.

'They're still looking *nervous*,' said Howard, peering at them. 'No need for *nerves!*' he said bracingly, again. 'We're all going to have a nice, relaxing holiday.'

'We certainly are,' said Purvis. 'Ortrud wants to go snorkelling and Allen would like to try golf.'

'Excellent,' said Howard. 'And I'm going to take you all to see the Armitage Museum.'

'Oh,' said Purvis. 'Yes.'

'Did you know,' said Howard, 'the Armitage Museum was founded by my great-great-great-great-great-great grandmother's second cousin once removed, Miss Hortence-Howardenia Armitage?'

'*Mmm,*' said Mickey Thompson. 'You told us.'

'The Armitage Museum,' continued Howard, 'contains Armitage-related memorabilia from around the world,

including 392 photocopies of
the birth, marriage and death
certificates of Armitages past,
and 64 newspaper cuttings.'

'That's *lovely*, Howard,' said
Purvis, stifling a yawn.

'It has the **largest**
collection of…

wait a minute,' said Howard,
staring at Allen and Ortrud,
who had curled up and closed
their eyes.

'What's wrong with them now?'

'Flying nerves, Howard,' said Purvis. '*Err*, shouldn't we be getting along to **check in**?'

'You're right,' said Howard. He picked up his bag and started rummaging in it. 'I'll just find my ticket and passport and stuff and oh dear.'

'What's wrong?' said Purvis.

'I've just had a thought,' said

Howard. He **d**
**r**
**o**
**p**
**p**
**e**
**d** his bag and sprinted off across the vast departure hall,

swerving to avoid a luggage trolley and vaulting a row of seats.

'Where's he going? What's he doing?' said Allen, jolting upright.

'I've no idea,' said Purvis.

'I have,' said Mickey Thompson. 'He's limbering up for the flight, of course. Come

on.' He put down his sombrero
and started to star-jump, so
Allen and Ortrud joined in
while Purvis watched Howard
head northwards, then
leftwards, grab a handful of
leaflets from a leaflet display,
then turn and run towards them.

'Right,' said Howard, arriving back, and opening a leaflet marked, "*Rules and Regulations, part 17(b), appendix 5, W-Z*". 'I need to work out what to do next.'

'**Check in** next, surely?' said Purvis.

'No, **press-ups** next,' said Mickey Thompson, plonking to the ground and attempting a **press-up**. Allen and

Ortrud plonked too and joined in. Howard gazed at them, confusedly.

'They're limbering up,' explained Purvis. 'For the flight.'

'I wish they wouldn't,' said Howard. 'It's distracting.'

'That's enough pressing-up

for now, actually,' puffed Mickey Thompson, rolling onto his back

and lying flat on the floor.
Allen and Ortrud rolled too
and
lay next to him.

'So, Howard,' said Purvis. 'Is
there a problem?'

'Yes,' said Howard. 'I'd
completely forgotten there
are all sorts of **rules and
regulations** about getting
through **check in** and
**security** and over to
**airside**.' He pointed at the
double doors in the distance.

Everyone looked at the doors and then at Howard.

'What sort of **rules and regulations**?' asked Purvis.

'We're not allowed any **wildlife**,' said Howard.

'That's OK, we haven't got any **wildlife**,' said Purvis as Ortrud

# trumpeted,

wildly.

Howard winced, and passed Purvis the leaflet.

'*Hmm,*' said Purvis, reading it out. 'It says,

"For the purposes of these rules and regulations wildlife is defined as any unauthorised animal including hedgehogs, donkeys, tigers, snakes——"'

'Ortrud's in the clear!' **cheered** Mickey Thompson.

'I haven't finished yet,' said Purvis. "*Badgers, foxes, elephants—*"

'Whoops,' said Mickey Thompson, as Ortrud **trumpeted** again even more wildly.

"*Cows*," continued Purvis, "*wombats etc.; mice*".'

Everyone gasped.

'But we're not **wild**,' said Mickey Thompson. 'We live in Howard's office; it's all cosy, with biscuits.'

'I know that and you know that,' said Howard, 'but the airport authorities don't. They'll say elephants and mice are **wild** things and that **wild** things are strictly against the rules. I'm not sure about Allen, either.'

Allen wagged his tail and his tongue lolled out.

'Allen's the least **wild** of any of us,' said Purvis. 'He won't be any trouble.'

'Of course he won't,'

said Howard, patting Allen's head.

'Nor will we,' said Mickey Thompson, brightly.

'Of course you w…' began Howard and stopped, and coughed. He walked over to some seats and sat down.

'I don't know what I was thinking,' he said. 'They're never going to let me through with a dog, two mice and an elephant.'

'Oh dear,' said Purvis.

'Ah well,' said Howard, 'never mind. I've managed without a holiday for – how **long** is it now?'

Purvis opened his bag and took out a piece of paper covered in pencil marks. He counted them up.

'Seven years, five months, three days,' he said.

'Then I can probably manage a little **longer**,' said Howard. 'We'd better get back to the office.'

'Howard!' chorused the
mice, disappointedly.

'But our holiday, Howard,'
said Mickey Thompson. 'We
were going to fly.'

'And snorkel,' said Purvis,
'and go to the beach, and
play golf and, and… visit the
Armitage Museum.'

Howard Sighed sadly and
the mice exchanged glances
then huddled together,
whispering.

41

'What's all the whispering?' said
Howard.

'*Err,*' said Purvis.

'*Go on*,' whispered Mickey
Thompson.

'The thing is,' said Purvis.

'What is the thing?' said
Howard.

'*Say it*,' whispered Mickey
Thompson.

'*Um,*' said Purvis,
swallowing. 'Would you prefer
it if we didn't come?'

Howard **narrowed** his eyes.

'*Hmm...*' he said. 'Would I prefer it if you didn't come, you say?'

The mice nodded.

'If you didn't have us you wouldn't have any problems,' said Purvis, 'and you could still go and see your museum.'

'Well, let me think…' said Howard, so the mice stared at the ground and shuffled a bit while Howard pretended to think.

. . . . . . . . . . . . . . . . . . . . . . . . . . . . . . . .

. . . . . . . . . . . . . . . . . . . . . . . . . . . . . . . .

'Howard?' said Purvis, after a while.

'OF COURSE I WOULDN'T PREFER IT IF YOU DIDN'T COME!' **shouted** Howard, leaping up. 'I've never heard such nonsense.'

'But—' began Purvis.

'But nothing,' said Howard.

'That settles it: one way or
another I'm going on holiday
and you're all coming with me.
Is that understood?'

Purvis let out a Sigh of relief
and Mickey Thompson started
to star-jump again in double
quick time, so everyone else
joined in.

'That's enough jumping for now, actually,' puffed Howard, quite quickly.

'We still need to work out how to get through without anyone noticing, not to mention the—'

'*Mr Bullerton,*' whispered Purvis.

'We're not taking him,' said Howard, 'and for once he needn't worry us; he's safely tucked away inside the office.'

'Oh no he's isn't,' **muttered** Mickey Thompson.

'LOOK OUT!'

**shouted** Purvis, and the
mice and Allen and Ortrud shot
under the seat just in time as Mr
Bullerton, Howard's **angry** boss,
arrived.

He was dragging a shiny suitcase
and wearing some stripey shorts,
and looking even **angrier** than
usual.

★

'Hello there,' said Howard,
trying to sound friendly.

**'GRRR-RRR,'**

said Mr Bullerton. 'What do
you think you're doing, Howard
Armitage?'

'I'm going on holiday,' said
Howard.

'Oh no you're not,'

said Mr Bullerton.

'But, but you said I could,'
said Howard.

'But, but I've changed my

mind,' said Mr Bullerton, in a sneery voice. 'I've decided I am the one who shall have a holiday and you are the one who shall work. Get back to the office.'

'No,' said Howard.

# 'WHAT?'

**roared** Mr Bullerton, turning puce.

'I couldn't possibly, I'm afraid,' said Howard. 'They're all far too excited.'

'They?' said Mr Bullerton.

'All? And wait, what's this?' He bent down and picked up Mickey Thompson's sombrero, which was lying nearby. *'Pah,'* he said, sniffing it. 'It's the one off that stupid straw souvenir donkey you keep on your desk.'

Howard gazed at it. 'Oh, so it is,' he said. 'I wondered where he got it from.'

'You're **burbling**,'

said Mr Bullerton, and he flapped the hat in Howard's face then dropped it and kicked it across the departure hall. There was a *spluttering* noise from underneath the seat.

'That was most unnecessary,' said Howard.

'Get back to work,' said Mr Bullerton. 'AND TAKE YOUR TINY SOMBRERO WITH YOU.'

He grabbed

Howard and Howard's bag and manhandled them over to the exit.

'STAY THERE,' *yelled* Howard, over his shoulder. 'I'LL BE BACK SOON.'

'Oh no,' said Purvis.

'Poor Howard,' said Allen.

'MY HAT,' *spluttered* Mickey Thompson. 'Did you see what he did? He kicked my hat.'

'Yes,' said Purvis. 'It was most unnecessary.'

'I'm going to find it,' said Mickey Thompson, and before anyone could do anything he shot out from under the seat and hurtled off.

'WAIT,' *yelled* Purvis, but it was too late — Mickey Thompson had already **disappeared** into the throng of trolleys and luggage and legs.

'Oh no,' said Purvis.

'Poor Mickey Thompson,' said Allen.

'I'll go and find him,' said Purvis, and he shot out from under the seat and hurtled off in the same direction.

'STAY WHERE YOU ARE,' he **shouted** over his shoulder. 'WE'LL BE BACK SOON.'

'WAIT,' *yelled* Allen,
and Ortrud **trumpeted**
in alarm, shot out from under
the seat and hurtled off in the *wrong direction.*

'*Ooh-err,*' said Allen,
dithering. '*Err-ooh,
um...* help.' He crept out

from under the seat, ran one way,

ran the other way,

dithered a little bit more and

hurtled off in a *different wrong direction.*

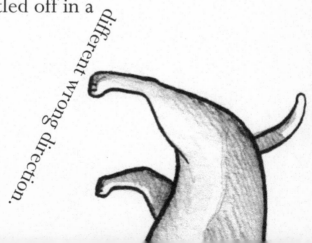

Meanwhile, Purvis was racing along frantically dodging wheels and feet and had started gaining on Mickey Thompson when there was a sudden **kerfuffle** up ahead. Mickey Thompson *skidded* to a **halt** and Purvis crashed into him just as a ride-on electric cart ***zoomed*** past, with a woman on top, being chased by a pack of photographers. In the middle of the flashing and clicking, the cart gave a lurch and stopped dead.

'Oh boy,' said the woman.

# 'BANGY!'

*yelled* the photographers. 'Purvis!' gasped Mickey Thompson, grabbing Purvis's arm. 'Look! It's Bangy de Gamba!'

'*Who?*' said Purvis.

'You know,' said Mickey Thompson, 'the one from that film we watched last week:

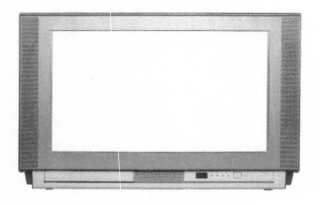

"*Mega-Collider Five*". She was the *Beautiful* scientist.'

'Oh,' said Purvis, peering.
'Oh, so it is. She's very, um…'
'*Beautiful*,' sighed
Mickey Thompson, 'and clever;
she was the one who discovered
the quark-gluon
plasma, remember?'

'Not really,' said Purvis, 'and anyway it wasn't her.'

'It was,' said Mickey Thompson, 'just after the man in the mustard suit turned out to be a baddie.'

'Yes, OK, well anyway,' said Purvis, 'we should get going.'

'No, wait,' said Mickey Thompson. 'Let's watch, just for a little while. I've never seen a famous star before.'

'I thought you wanted to find your hat,' said Purvis.

'*Mmm,*' said Mickey Thompson, entranced, so together they watched as Bangy de Gamba climbed off the cart and did dazzling and twirling for the photographers while her driver tried to start it up again and her heavies hovered *nervously* nearby.

'BANGY! BANGY!' *yelled* the photographers.

'Something's stuck,' **muttered** the driver.

'Unstick it,' gritted Bangy, dazzling and twirling harder and faster as more and more people realised what was going on and gathered around to gawp.

'*Wow,*' breathed Mickey Thompson.

'Yes,' said Purvis.

'*Ah-ha,*' said the driver, yanking out something from one of the wheels, and flapping it.

'My hat,' gasped Mickey Thompson.

'What is it?' said Bangy.

'IT'S MY HAT,' called Mickey Thompson, waving his hand in the air and hopping up and down.

'It's just some bit of old rubbish,' the driver told Bangy. 'I'll bin it as soon as we find a bin.'

Mickey Thompson made a *spluttering* noise.

'No, don't do that,' said Bangy. 'Look, it's a tiny sombrero. It's cute!'

Mickey Thompson made a **gurgling** noise.

'I think I'll keep it for luck,' she said, and she popped it into her bag, climbed on the cart and was *whizzed* away.

Mickey Thompson made a yodelling noise and launched himself through the photographers onto the back of the cart and was *whizzed* away too.

'NOOOOOOO!' *yelled* Purvis, as the electric cart shot past **check in**, was waved through **security** and **disappeared** in the distance through the double doors to **airside**.

# Knickers

**Purvis**

watched the photographers and onlookers d i s p e r s e and then hurried back to the seat to find Allen and Ortrud. They were nowhere to be seen.

He watched the people coming and going across the $vast$ departure hall and was starting to feel lonely, and a little afraid, when Howard rushed up.

'PURVIS!' he **shouted**. 'Thank goodness you're all still… *Aagh!*'

'I know,' said Purvis, 'I'm sorry: I don't know where they are.'

'But I said "wait here",' said Howard. 'Why didn't they wait?'

'Mickey Thompson went to find his sombrero and I went to find Mickey Thompson, but he got *whizzed* through to **airside** on Bangy de Gamba's electric cart and I didn't know what to do,' said Purvis, unhappily. 'Then when I came back to find Allen and Ortrud they'd **disappeared** too.'

'*What* cart?' said Howard. 'Was it some kind of novelty ride or something?'

'No, it's a proper cart with a driver and everything,' said Purvis. 'It jammed stuck on Mickey Thompson's hat and she kept it as a lucky charm. She's famous.'

'Who is?' said Howard.

'Bangy de Gamba,' said Purvis.

'*Who?*' said Howard.

'You know,' said Purvis, 'the *Beautiful* scientist from "*Mega-Collider Five*". Mickey Thompson took a shine to her

and the next thing I knew…'
Purvis made a *whooshing*
gesture towards the double
doors. 'Gone,' he said.
'Where's Mr Bullerton?'

'Gone too, for now,' said
Howard. 'I gave him the slip,
but he'll be around here
somewhere so we need to be
careful because—'

'Listen,' said Purvis.

'I'm talking,' said Howard.
'We need to be careful
because—'

'They're saying something about a dog,' said Purvis, bouncing, as an announcement echoed around the hall.

'—og,' it ended.

'What did it say?' What did it say?' said Howard.

'Come on!' said Purvis, *sprinting* off.

'WHERE ARE WE GOING?' *yelled* Howard, *sprinting* after him. 'WAIT FOR MEEEEEE!'

★

Purvis raced westwards then took a sharp right,

nipped through a narrow gap between some suitcases and emerged in front of a door marked

'Lost Property Office'.

'Steady on,' said a woman,
as Howard crashed breathlessly
into the cases and landed heavily
on top of one. It was **large**,
and hard, and tartan.

'Ouch,' said Howard.
'You've burst it,' said the
woman. 'You've burst my bag.'

'Sorry,' said Howard, trying to stuff some voluminous frilly **Knickers** back inside.

'Let go,' said the woman, grabbing them.

'I'm trying to help,' said Howard, grabbing them back. 'I...*whoops*.'

'You've ripped them!' shrieked the woman. 'Help! Somebody help!'

'What's going on?' said
a familiar voice. It was Mr
Bullerton.

**'YOU!'** he **roared**.

'Oh, hello again,' said
Howard, trying to sound
friendly.

'He burst my bag,' said the
woman. 'He jumped on top and
burst it and now he's ripping up
my clothes.'

'How dare you?' said Mr
Bullerton, in a steely voice.

'I didn't mean to,' said Howard. 'It was an accident.'

'Put down this poor woman's undergarments at once,' said Mr Bullerton.

'I don't want them,' said Howard, pushing them at the woman.

'Nor do I, now,' said the woman, pushing them back.

'And I don't want YOU,' said Mr Bullerton. 'GET BACK TO WORK.' He jammed the **Knickers** on Howard's head like a frilly hat and manhandled him over to the exit.

Purvis winced, and Slipped inside the **Lost Property Office**. He tiptoed past a man snoozing in a chair and, just as he'd hoped, found Allen, sprawled on a rug with a plate of biscuits, watching television. 'Allen!' said Purvis. 'I...*oh!*' He stared at the screen.

'Have you seen this film?' said Allen. 'It's very exciting, the *Beautiful* scientist is—'

'Here! In this airport!' said
Purvis. 'She's got Mickey
Thompson and we have to find
him and get him back!'

Allen dropped his biscuit.
'But how? But why?' he said. 'I
thought she was a goodie.'

'It all happened because
she liked Mickey Thompson's
sombrero,' said Purvis. 'Oh,
Allen, what are we going to do?'

'Don't worry, we'll think of
something,' said Allen. '*Ooh!* I
know!'

84

'What? What?' said Purvis.

'Let's have a biscuit,' said Allen, passing Purvis the plate.

'Thanks,' said Purvis, taking one. Allen took one too and nibbled it, worriedly.

'Did I hear Mr Bullerton **shouting** again?' he asked.

'Yes, he was **angry** with Howard for **bursting** a bag and *ripping* some—' Purvis coughed and went a bit **pink**.

'Some what?' said Allen.

'**Knickers,**' whispered Purvis. 'He put them on Howard's head and marched him off.'

Allen choked on his biscuit and someone started hammering at the door.

'I'll go and see who it is,' said Purvis, and he *slid out* of the **Lost Property Office** and found Howard waiting impatiently.

'You've taken off your *pretty* hat,' said Purvis, brightly.

'Don't push your luck,' said
Howard. 'Is Allen in there?'

'Yes, but I couldn't see
Ortrud. You'd better ask, just in
case.'

'I can't,' said Howard, 'they'll
think I've gone completely—
Hello!'

'Hello,' said the lost property
man, emerging, and yawning.

'I've come to collect my dog,'
said Howard.

'One moment,' said the
lost property man, and he

**disappeared** and came back with Allen. 'One dog,' he said, handing him over. '*Sign* here, please.'

'Thanks,' said Howard, *signing*.

'*Ask him,*' **hissed** Purvis.

'*I can't,*' **hissed** Howard.

'There's no such word as can't,' said the lost property man, with a wink.

'Right, OK,' said Howard. 'Well, I was just wondering whether anything else had been left here today.'

'Lots,' said the lost property man.

'One wallet,
one coat,
one book,
one shoe,
nine umbrellas
and a packet
of sandwiches:
liverwurst ones.
They're past the sell-by date.
Want them?'

'No, thank you,' said Howard. 'I was after something a little more—'

'Tasty?' said the lost property man.

'Unusual,' said Howard.

'Liverwurst's fairly unusual,' said the lost property man.

'I meant unusual as in more like an elephant,' said Howard, trying to sound casual.

'Not today,' said the lost property man, cheerfully. 'If you'd asked yesterday it would have been a different matter. We were crawling with elephants yesterday: pink ones, blue ones, some of them covered in **stripes**.' He laughed, **loudly**.

'Yes, thank you,' said Howard, bundling Allen and Purvis away.

★

'What did he mean?' asked Purvis.

'I don't know,' said Howard, 'but I'm exhausted already and we haven't even been on holiday yet. I told you he'd think I was odd to ask for an elephant.'

'Never mind,' said Purvis.
'We've got Allen back and
now we know Ortrud isn't
THERE! THERE!'
'WHERE?
*WHOOPS!*' said Howard,
nearly over balancing as
something **small** and elephant-
shaped shot past and scooted
away.

'That wasn't Ortrud,' said
Howard.
'WATCH OUT!

# HERE COMES ANOTHER ONE!' *yelled* Purvis.

'Eek,' said Howard, leaping out of the way as something else clattered past.

'That wasn't her either,' said Purvis. 'That was a dinosaur, on wheels.'

'What's going on?' groaned Howard, rubbing his head.

'Ooh, I think I can see her,' said Purvis, *sprinting* off. 'Come on!'

'Not again,' groaned Howard, picking up Allen and t$_o$tt$_e$r$_{i}n_g$ after him.

Purvis raced across the departure hall in a southerly direction, zig-zagging round trolleys,

scootling between feet and keeping an eye out for women with **large** tartan cases.

'**Wait**,' panted Howard. 'I can't········ keep········ up.'

Purvis *skidded* to a **halt**.

'We're too late, anyway.

Look,' he said, pointing into

the distance. They all stood and

watched as the double doors

to **airside** opened and in

went a woman followed by a

boy of about twelve followed by
a girl of about nine followed by
a boy of about six followed by
a man of about forty pulling a
girl of about three on a ride-on
suitcase shaped like an elephant
followed closely by Ortrud.

'Clever Ortrud!' said Purvis. 'She disguised herself as a suitcase and got through.'

'Two down, three to go,' said Howard, pocketing Purvis and re-tucking Allen under his arm. 'Come along,' he said. 'Our holiday beckons.'

Purposefully, he marched
up to the double doors and
was immediately stopped by
**security**.

'Wave us through, please,'
said Howard.

'Is this your dog, sir?' said the
security guard, looking at Allen.

'This dog is a film star,' said
Howard, and Allen
and Purvis gasped.
'He's part of the
entourage of Miss
Bangy de Gamba.'

'The *Beautiful* scientist
from "*Mega-Collider Five*",' said
the security guard.

'The very one,' said Howard.

'Through you go, then,' said
the security guard, and he
stepped aside and
stepped back again, quickly.

'Just a minute,' he said.
'There was no dog in
"*Mega-Collider Five*".'

'Are you sure about that?'
said Howard.

'Completely: I've seen it nine times; it's one of my favourites.'

'I see,' said Howard. 'Well…'

The security guard *raised* an eyebrow. 'Well?' he said.

'Well…' said Howard.

'"*Mega-Collider Six*",' *hissed* Purvis.

'*Ah-ha!*' said Howard. 'Yes! *Well*, as you're a fan you'll be interested to learn that "*Mega-Collider Six*" will be even better than the other five because this dog's going to be in it.'

The security guard regarded Allen speculatively.

'What part does he play?' he asked. 'I can't see how a dog would fit with the story so far.'

'Oh, really?' said Howard. 'Well…'

The security guard raised his other eyebrow.

'*He chases the man in the mustard suit,*' **hissed** Purvis.

'Mustard suit?' *spluttered* Howard.

102

'**Ooh!**' said the security guard. 'He's a stunt dog, is he?'

Exactly,' said Howard.

'Thought he must be,' said the security guard, sounding impressed. 'Did you see the bit where mustard-suit man gets dangled out of a helicopter on a flimsy rope and plunges into shark-infested waters far beneath?'

Allen gave a GULP.
'And the bit where he leaps
from the roof of a speeding
train onto the roof of another

speeding train and slips and
catapults down a mountainside
into a snake-filled ravine?
Is that the kind of thing the
dog'll be doing?'

'Absolutely,' said Howard.

Allen twisted around and
gazed up at Howard with
**large** and worried-
looking eyes.

'Through you go then,' said
the security guard, waving them
through the double doors to
**airside**.

'Marvellous,' **muttered** Howard.

'We made it!' **cheered** Purvis.

'I'll radio Miss de Gamba's team and let them know you're coming,' called the security guard, un-clipping his walkie-talkie.

## 'NO!'

**shouted** Howard.
'DON'T DO THAT!'

But the double doors had already clunked shut behind them.

They found themselves in a **large** bright space filled with busy shops and people milling about and buying things.

'*Purvis,*' whispered Allen.

'*Oh!*' said Purvis, gazing around. 'This isn't what I was expecting.'

'What were you expecting?' said Howard.

'Sky and clouds, not shops and MICKEY THOMPSON!!!'

'I can't see him,' said Howard.

'Under there,' said
Purvis, pointing at a
**large** cardboard
sweet dangling from
the ceiling, with
the words

"Pic
'n'
Mix"

written on
it. Under the
cardboard
sweet was
a stall selling all sorts of real sweets

and underneath that stood Mickey Thompson, looking hungry. He jumped when he heard his name and gave a genial wave.

'Hello, there,' he said, strolling over. 'Howard, can we get some of those big red ones please and some chewy bananas, some white chocolate buttons, err, two or three of those stripey ones there and maybe some—'

'Where have you been?'

interrupted Howard. 'You mustn't run off like that.'

'I didn't, I rode on a cart. It was brilliant! I've been in there.'

He pointed at a smart-looking door with a smart-looking *sign* that said: "**BRABAZON LOUNGE**".

'It's all sort of… *golden*,' he said, 'There are armchairs and flowers and a swimming pool with a fountain, and mermaids, and waiters walking about with

plates of strawberry tarts.'

'No!' said Purvis.

'Yes!' said Mickey Thompson.

'Can I see?' said Purvis.

'I'll show you, come on,' said Mickey Thompson, *trotting* off.

'STOP!' *yelled* Howard, and Mickey Thompson *trotted* back again.

'Look at the sign,' said Howard. 'That lounge is for

**VIPS AND FIRST CLASS PASSENGERS ONLY.**

That's not us.'

'But Howard,' said Purvis.

'But nothing,' said Howard.

'But Bangy de Gamba says…'

'Never mind her,' said Howard, checking his watch. 'We're supposed to set off in less than an hour and we don't want any more mishaps, do we?'

'No, Howard,' said the mice.

'No, Howard,' agreed
Howard. 'Let's aim to avoid film
stars and bosses.'

'And tartan suitcases,'
**muttered** Purvis.

'Quite,' said Howard. 'All we
need to do now is find Ortrud
and go away on holiday.'

'FLY away,' said
Mickey Thompson,

**stretching**,

and breathing deeply.

'Ortrud's in the
**BRABAZON LOUNGE**, by
the way.'

'Oh no,' groaned Howard.

'Oh good,' said Purvis,
*trotting* off. 'I'll get her, shall
I?'

# 'STOP!'

*yelled* Howard.

Purvis came back again,
reluctantly.

'It's OK, Howard,' said

Mickey Thompson. 'Bangy de Gamba says—'

'Shush,' said Howard. **'LOOK OUT!'** *yelled* Purvis, and the mice and Allen dived behind Howard just in time as Mr Bullerton loomed up.

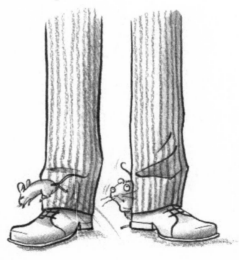

'SO!' said Mr Bullerton. 'You've done it this time.'

'What have I done?' said Howard.

Mr Bullerton took a piece of paper from his pocket, cleared his throat and began to read:

'*Press Release,*' (he read).

**'Mega-Collider *Miss narrowly misses mega-collision!***

*Miss Bangy de Gamba, star of the phenomenally popular* Mega-Collider *movies, was involved in a shocking incident at the airport today when someone kicked a toy sombrero at her, violently. Miraculously, she was unharmed, but the airport authorities are seeking the culprit and offering a reward for information.'*

'I saw you kick that hat and I'm going to hand you in,' said Mr Bullerton. 'No holiday for you, Howard Armitage. What have you got to say about that?'

# 'BRABAZON LOUNGE!'
*yelled* Howard.

'*Eh?*' said Mr Bullerton, but
he was too late: Howard and
the mice and Allen had already
bundled at top speed over to the
smart-looking door and were
scrabbling at it, frenziedly.

'WHAT
DO YOU
THINK
YOU'RE
DOING?'
**shouted** Mr Bullerton.
'YOU
CAN'T
GO
IN
THERE.'

'Watch me,' said Howard. He yanked the door open and they all rushed inside.

# 'This way!'

*yelled* Mickey Thompson, racing off, so they all raced after him past armchairs and mermaids and flowers and fountains and bumped straight into the tartan-suitcase woman, knocking her into the pool.

'So sorry,' called Howard as they thundered past hotly.

**'STOP HIM!'**

*yelled* the woman as she struggled out, wetly. 'THAT'S THE ONE WHO TRIED TO STEAL MY **KNICKERS**.'

'Did he indeed?' said the security guard, leaping out from a doorway. *'Ah-ha!* It's you!'

'It isn't,' said Howard.

'It is,' said the security guard. *'EEK!'* said everyone else as Howard *tripped* over an elephant-suitcase and upset

several trays of

strawberry tarts.

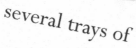

'Back the other way!' *yelled* Mickey Thompson, racing off again, so they all raced after him past fountains and flowers and mermaids and armchairs and bumped straight into Mr Bullerton.

'*Ah-ha!*' he said, grabbing Howard's wrist. 'I have you now.'

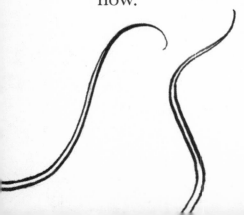

# Drummond and the nose cones, part 1

**H**oward *wrenched* himself free from Mr Bullerton's grip and *yelled* 'RUN!'

so they ran, straight up a wide
white corridor into a coffee
shop and out again, scattering
cup-cakes and flecks of foam.

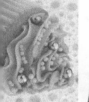

Veering wildly from left to right
they crashed through bookshops
and clothes shops and bag

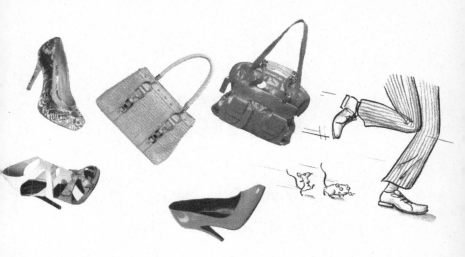

shops and shoe shops, smashed
several bottles in the perfume
emporium and, heady with
musk and bluebells, swerved
down a different corridor and
crashed through that too.

# 'COME BACK HERE!'

**roared** Mr Bullerton, closely.

*'Yikes!'* said everyone, scaredly, and they dived in the nearest doorway marked "LADIES", shot back out and continued down the corridor,

under

a bridge, up some stairs

130

and burst through a door into a
silent room with a giant map of
the world, all blues and greens
and **shimmering** with
hundreds and thousands of tiny
lights. Purvis stopped.

'Wow,' he said.

'DON'T
STOP!'

*yelled* Howard and they all
set off again out of the room,
down a ramp, through a tunnel
and outside onto a flat and
windy piece of land.

'I think we've managed to lose him,' **PUFFED** Howard.

'Good, then let's go back in,' said Mickey Thompson. 'There was something in one of those shops I needed to look at.'

'And somehow we need to fetch Ortrud,' puffed Howard.

'Wait,' said Purvis. 'Listen.'

Everyone listened.

'All I can hear is Howard **PUFFING**,' said Mickey Thompson.

'Speak for yourself,' said Howard, offendedly, 'I... oh.'

Purvis was right: a distant thrum had become a

# thundering

roar and the sky was

# darkening.

'*Is it Mr Bullerton?*' whispered Allen.

'I don't think so,' said Purvis.

'I don't like it,' wailed Mickey Thompson.

'EXCUSE ME', called a voice from the sky.

'Howard!'

squeaked the mice, as the

roar got even

thunderier

and the sky turned

darker

still.

'HERE I COME!' called the voice,
'YOU MIGHT WANT TO JUST...'

'DUCK!'

**shouted** Howard, and
everyone ducked just in time

as a little plane *whooshed* down narrowly missing the tops of their heads, landed with a thump and clattered along rather fast.

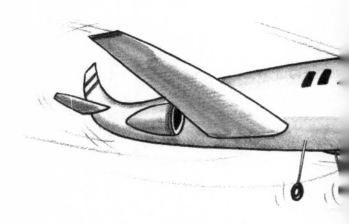

'WHEE!' said the plane as it swerved and *skidded* and bumped into the side of the airport, nose cone first, with a crunching noise.

'Bother,' said the plane. 'There goes another one.'

'Quick,' said Howard, 'let's get out of here ***fast*** before someone finds us and… oh dear.'

'*Yoo-hoo,*' said a pilot, running up. 'Thank goodness you got here so quickly.'

'Err,' said Howard. 'Yes!'

'We take off in less than an hour. Will you have enough time?'

'Err,' said Howard. 'Yes?'

'**Phew,**' said the pilot. 'Where is she?'

'Um, over, err…' Howard wafted his hand in the general direction of the airport.

'Ah,' said the pilot. 'Good. I'll leave you to get on with it then.'

'It?' said Howard.

'Yes,' said the pilot.

'It being?' said Howard.

'Fixing the plane, of course,' said the pilot, giving Howard a funny look. 'Hurry up! Miss de Gamba won't want to be kept waiting. We're all depending on you.'

Howard made a **gargling** noise as the pilot strode away.

'What am I going to do now?' he said, panickedly.

'Fix the plane?' suggested Purvis.

'But I don't know how,' said Howard.

'Why's that then?' asked Mickey Thompson.

'Surprisingly enough the need's never arisen, what with me not being an aeroplane engineer and everything.'

'Steady, Howard,' said Purvis.
'I'm sure we can sort something
out. I'll **pop up** and have a
little chat.'

'Who with?' said Howard.

'The plane – he'll probably be
able to give us a few pointers.'

'Eh?' said Howard.

'You know,' said Purvis.
'Hints and tips.'

'Good idea,' said Mickey
Thompson. 'I'll come too.'

'No, you wait here with
Howard,' said Purvis. 'Look at

him – he's all upset.'

'Pop up and pointers, tips?'
said Howard, **burbling**.
'They're all depending on me.'

Mickey Thompson patted
Howard, reassuringly.

'Don't worry,'
said Allen.
'I'll look after
him. You two
go and see
what you can
find out.'

'OK,' said Purvis. 'Come on, you.' He jumped onto the wheel of the plane, hoicked Mickey Thompson up and together they climbed along a wing, over the fuselage and onto the nose cone to introduce themselves.

'*Lovely* to meet you too,' said the plane, once they had. 'I'm Drummond. How does it look?' He wiggled his nose cone and the mice studied it.

'It is quite crumpled,' said Purvis.

'I thought it might be,' said
Drummond.

'Does it hurt?' asked Mickey
Thompson, giving it a gentle
prod.

'Not in the least,' said
Drummond, 'but I'm going to
be in trouble. Again.'

'Has it happened before?'
asked Purvis.

'It happens all the time,' said
Drummond. 'This is the
ninety-ninth nose cone I've
broken this year.'

'Drummond!' said Mickey
Thompson, sounding
impressed.

'The thing is, I've only one
chance left,' said Drummond,

worriedly. 'If I reach a hundred the airport authorities will ground me for good.'

'Tell them it was our fault,' said Purvis. 'We were in the way and put you off.'

'But you didn't,' said Drummond. 'I'm just not very good at landings.'

'Ah,' said Purvis.

'Or take-offs.'

'I see,' said Purvis.

'I'm all right in the middle bits.'

'There you are then!' said Purvis, encouragingly.

'As long as I don't have to go too high; I'm not that keen on heights because they make me feel queasy.'

'That's unfortunate, in the circumstances,' said Purvis. 'Have you ever considered a change of career?'

'Gosh, no,' said Drummond. 'I love flying; it's wonderful *whooshing* along through the air with the birds and clouds.'

'Ooooh,' said Mickey
Thompson, dreamily. 'Do
clouds taste
like candyfloss?'

'Not really,' said Drummond.
Mickey Thompson looked
bitterly disappointed.

'I meant to say not usually,' said Drummond, quickly. 'You only get the full flavour at certain times of the year when the weather conditions are exactly right.'

'What times, when?' said Mickey Thompson.

'Drummond probably isn't allowed to say,' said Purvis.

'Actually, it's impossible to know in advance when it's going to happen,' said Drummond, 'which means it comes as a pleasant and rare surprise.'

'Ahhh,' Sighed Mickey
Thompson, happily.

'Yup,' said Drummond,
'flying's great. It's me that's the
problem, what with the heights,
and the take-offs, and the—'

'Landings and feeling queasy,'
finished Purvis, nodding. 'Right,
how can we help?'

'You can tell me this,' said
Drummond. 'On a scale of
nought to five, with nought
being "not at all" and five being

"extremely", how crumpled
would you say my nose cone is?'

'Hmm,' said Purvis, studying
it again, carefully. 'I'd say it's
about a—'

'Six,' blurted out Mickey
Thompson, and Purvis shushed
him.

'You can't have six,' he whispered. 'Drummond said go up to five: five for extremely.'

'Six for mega-extremely,' said Mickey Thompson. 'Or seven for double-extremely. Or EIGHT for I've never seen anything like it in my life.'

Drummond gave a start. 'Is it as bad as that?' he said.

'No,' said Purvis.

'Yes,' said Mickey Thompson, and they started a **small** scuffle.

'Is everything all right?' called
Drummond, as they scuffled
themselves across his nose cone
and onto the top of his head.

'Sorry, Drummond,' said
Purvis, as they scrambled back
down again. 'We've agreed to
settle for four.'

'And a half,' said Mickey
Thompson.

'Four,' said Purvis, firmly, 'for
very crumpled.'

'In that case it's too noticeable
and will have to be replaced,'

said Drummond. 'There should
be some spares in that aircraft
hangar next to the airport. Do
you think you could manage to
bring me one?'

'We'll try,' said Purvis.

'Quick as you can, then,' said
Drummond. 'There
isn't much time.'

So as quickly as they could,
Purvis and Mickey Thompson
clambered back over the

fuselage, slithered along the
wing and

**bounced off**

the wheel onto Allen, who was
lying on his back gazing up at
the sky, looking serious.

Howard was solidly asleep beside him.

'**Oof**,' said Allen, as they landed on his stomach.

'ATTENTION! ATTENTION! WE'VE DETECTED AN URGENT DAMAGE SCENARIO, CATEGORY FOUR AND A HALF,' **shouted** Mickey Thompson, pretending to be a lab assistant from *Mega-Collider Five*.

Purvis shushed him. 'Hush,' he said. 'Howard's sleeping.'

'OOPS,'

said Mickey Thomspon.

'Category four and a half?' whispered Allen, struggling upright. 'What does it mean?'

'It means we need a new nose cone,' said Purvis, setting off. 'Come on.'

157

The three of them left Howard snoring and hurried over to the giant aircraft hangar, which was full of gangways and cranes and pieces of plane but had, as far as they could find, no nose cones.

'Drummond must have been mistaken,' said Purvis.

'Oh no,' groaned Mickey Thompson. 'What if he's used them all up? He probably muddled the numbers and thought he was only on ninety nine when he'd already reached a hundred.'

'In which case,' said Purvis,
'he's used his last chance too.'

'He'll never f{ly} again and
taste the clouds,' wailed Mickey
Thompson. 'He's going to be so
upset.'

'He's not the only one,'
said Purvis. 'Drummond
was supposed to f{ly} Bangy
de Gamba, remember, and
if he can't neither can she so
Howard'll be in trouble for not
fixing him, which he couldn't,

and for kicking the hat, which he didn't, and for saying Allen's a film star, which he isn't, and you know what that means, don't you?'

Allen and Mickey Thompson shook their heads, *confusedly*.

'It means we won't be going away on holiday.'

'Um,' said Allen.

'flying away,' said Mickey Thompson, **slumping** to the ground. 'Oh, I really, really wanted to.'

'So did I,' said Purvis, **slumping** too.

'Err,' said Allen.

'What's up, Allen?' asked Purvis.

'Did you just say I'm *not* a film star?' said Allen.

'Yes, Allen,' said Purvis. 'Of course you're not.'

'So I won't need to do any stunts then, will I?' said Allen.

'No, Allen,' said Purvis. 'Of course you won't. I hope you're not too—'

'I'M SO HAPPY!'
*yelled* Allen, bouncing.

'…disappointed,' finished Purvis.

'This is the best thing that's ever happened to me,' said Allen, running around in a circle.

'I didn't know the film star thing was worrying you,' said Purvis. 'I wish you'd said.'

'I didn't like to,' said Allen. 'It's such a relief!'

The mice sat and watched

him **b**ⁱ**o**ⁱ**u**ⁱ**n**ⁱ**c**ⁱ**e** away across the hangar and out of the door, then suddenly *skid* to a **halt** and turn, and run back.

'It's *them*,' he panted. 'They're there.'

The mice crept over to the door and peeped out. Allen was right: Mr Bullerton was lurking in one direction and the security guard was skulking in the other direction while, in the distance, Drummond was looking worried.

# Drummond and the nose cones, part 2

h, no,' groaned Mickey Thompson. 'What are we going to do now?'

'We must think of a plan,' said Purvis.

'Good idea,' said Mickey Thompson and he and Allen looked at Purvis expectantly.

'What?' said Purvis.

'Go on, then,' said Mickey Thompson.

'I said "*we*", not "*me*",' said Purvis.

'But you're clever at thinking up plans,' said Allen, and Mickey Thompson nodded.

'OK,' said Purvis. 'Give me a moment or two.'

So Purvis perched on a spare

aeroplane tyre to think while
Mickey Thompson ran about
with his arms sticking out,
**shouting** 'WHeeeeeeeeeeeeeeeeeeeeeeeeeeeee!'

and Allen kept a look out for wandering security guards and roving Mr Bullertons. After a moment or two Purvis leapt up and said, 'Got it!' and the others ran over.

'The plan is called "*Operation Nose Cone*",' announced Purvis, secretly pretending to be a clever and *Beautiful* scientist. 'First I shall summarise the facts. **Fact number one:** Drummond needs a new nose cone. Agreed?'

'Agreed,' said Mickey Thompson.

**'Fact number two:** we haven't got a new nose cone. Agreed?'

'Yes,' said Allen.

'Say "*agreed*",' whispered Mickey Thompson, nudging him.

'Sorry,' said Allen. 'Agreed.'

'And the plan is,' said Purvis, 'we use a disguise!'

Allen and Mickey Thompson looked at Purvis, blankly.

'Can you elaborate?' asked

Mickey Thompson.

'Instead of replacing it we cover it up and make it look like a high-spec-top-grade-supersonic-super-duper all round better kind of a nose cone,' said Purvis. 'Then no one will notice it's crumpled, no one will get into trouble and we can have our holiday.'

'Good plan!' said Mickey Thompson.

'Thank you,' said Purvis, taking a **small** bow.

'Yes, well done, Purvis,' said
Allen, and Purvis bobbed a
curtsey.

'But what shall we use?' asked
Mickey Thompson. 'There's
nothing suitable here.'

'We'll have to go back to the
airport and look in the shops,'
said Purvis.

'Um,' said Allen.

'Off we go,' said Mickey
Thompson, setting off
towards the door.

'Err,' said Allen.

'Let's hurry,' said Purvis, also setting off towards the door.

# 'STOP!'

*yelled* Allen,
and the mice
jumped, and

stopped.

'What about *them*,' whispered Allen. 'They might see us, and catch us.'

'Whoops,' said Purvis. 'I'd forgotten about *them*. Good point, Allen.'

'I know what we must do,' said Mickey Thompson.

'What?' said Purvis.

'We must think of a plan.'

'Go on, then,' said Purvis.

'I was hoping you might be able to fill in the details,' said Mickey Thompson. Purvis sighed and sat down on the spare aeroplane tyre and then leapt up again.

'GOT IT!' he **shouted**. 'WE USE A DISGUISE!'

Allen and Mickey Thompson looked at Purvis, confusedly.

'Isn't that the same as the other plan?' asked Mickey Thompson.

'Sort of,' admitted Purvis.

'So you want *us* to dress

176

up as top-grade-super-thingy nose cones, too?' asked Mickey Thompson.

'No,' said Purvis.

'I'm a little bit worried three nose cones walking about might attract *their* attention,' said Allen. 'It isn't something you see every day.'

'I know,' said Purvis. 'I——'

'And it won't work, anyway, Purvis,' said Mickey Thompson. 'We can't go to the shops without the disguise and we can't get the disguise without going to the shops.'

'I know,' said Purvis. 'I—'

'We're stuck,' sighed Mickey Thompson, sadly. 'Completely stuck.'

'WILL YOU PLEASE LISTEN TO ME!' said Purvis, rather **loudly**.

'We disguise ourselves as an aeroplane tyre, not nose cones, by hiding in this one here and rolling along in it. If Mr Bullerton and the security guard see an aeroplane tyre rolling along they'll think it's simply part of normal airport business.'

'Good plan!' said Mickey Thompson.

'Yes, very well done, Purvis,' said Allen, so they all climbed inside the spare aeroplane tyre and jiggled about until it started to roll, bumpily, out of the hanger, smoothly across the runway and extremely quickly down a slope to the airport.

'AAGHH!' they went as they picked up speed.

# 'AAGHH!'

went Mr Bullerton and the
security guard, leaping out of
the way.

'I feel dizzy,' groaned Allen.

'I feel sick,' said Mickey
Thompson.

# 'WE'RE GOING TOO FAST,' yelled

Purvis. 'We're going to—'

 went the tyre

into the side of the airport and
they all fell out and lay on the
grass, panting.

'Quick,' **PUFFED**
Purvis. 'We haven't got time
to lie around here.' So they all
struggled up and ran into the
tunnel, up the ramp,

through the room, down the
stairs, under the bridge and
back to the airport shops where
people were busy tidying,
re-stacking things and mopping
up spillages.

'It's very messy,' commented Purvis. 'I wonder why.'

'And I wonder what all this sticky stuff is over everything,' said Mickey Thompson, licking. 'Mmm! Coffee-shop cupcake!'

'Ah,' said Purvis. 'I think that might have been our fault.'

'It was Mr Bullerton's fault,' said Mickey Thompson. 'We wouldn't have knocked things over if he hadn't been chasing us.'

'True,' said Purvis. 'Right, we'd better start finding things to use for Drummond's disguise. Let's split up and meet back here in ten minutes, and remember to make a note of what comes from where so Howard can pay for it all afterwards.'

Nine minutes and 59 seconds later Purvis stood waiting. Stacked in a neat pile beside him was a **large** book entitled: "*Clouds: a spotter's guide*", an even **larger** book entitled: "*Advanced Aerodynamics*", a ball of string, a tin of travel sweets, a football, and a smart umbrella with the phrase: "*Fly me to the moon*" printed on it over and over again.

'Well, it wasn't doing any good just sitting around in that

Lost Property Office,' he told himself, as he *admired* it.

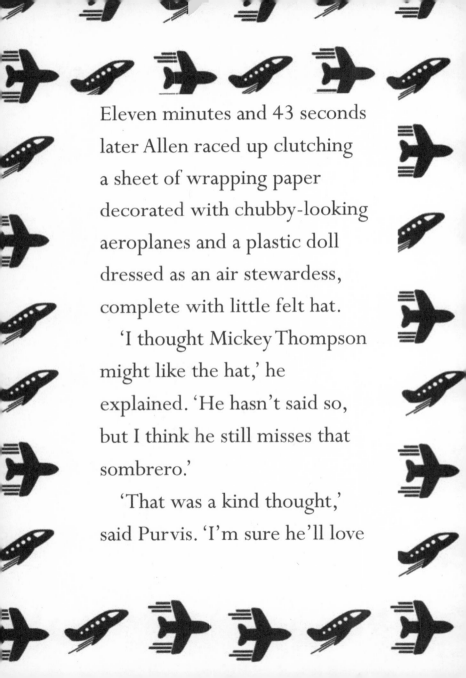

Eleven minutes and 43 seconds later Allen raced up clutching a sheet of wrapping paper decorated with chubby-looking aeroplanes and a plastic doll dressed as an air stewardess, complete with little felt hat.

'I thought Mickey Thompson might like the hat,' he explained. 'He hasn't said so, but I think he still misses that sombrero.'

'That was a kind thought,' said Purvis. 'I'm sure he'll love

it. Once he arrives.'

Seventeen minutes and 17
seconds later Mickey Thompson
raced up.

'Sorry I'm late,' he
**PUFFED**, 'I...oooh that's
a nice hat.'

'It's yours,' said Purvis.

'No!' said Mickey Thompson.

'Yes!' said Purvis. 'Allen got it
for you.'

So Mickey Thompson tried
on his hat and *dazzled* and

twirled for a pack of imaginary
photographers while Purvis
and Allen examined what
he'd collected: a spray can of
burnished gold paint, an apple
core, a long string of fairy
lights and a box of squashed
doughnuts in a variety of shapes
and flavours.

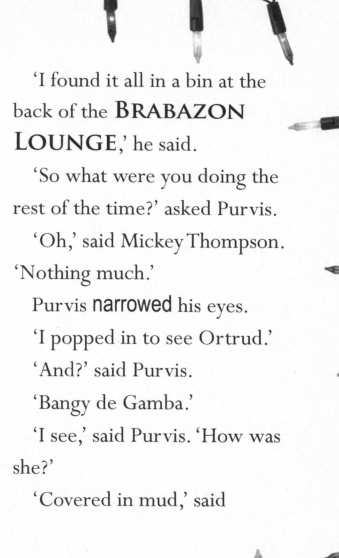

'I found it all in a bin at the back of the **BRABAZON LOUNGE**,' he said.

'So what were you doing the rest of the time?' asked Purvis.

'Oh,' said Mickey Thompson. 'Nothing much.'

Purvis narrowed his eyes.

'I popped in to see Ortrud.'

'And?' said Purvis.

'Bangy de Gamba.'

'I see,' said Purvis. 'How was she?'

'Covered in mud,' said

Mickey Thompson.

'Why?' gasped Purvis.

'What had happened?'

'She was having some kind of spa treatment beauty thing,' said Mickey Thompson.

'*Ortrud?*' said Purvis.

'No, Bangy de Gamba. Ortrud was in the swimming pool, practising snorkelling. She'd had about ten

strawberry tarts, too,' said
Mickey Thompson, sounding
put out. 'She ate them with
Bangy, for tea.'

'Did somebody mention tea?'
said Howard, looming up.

'AAGHH!'

*yelled* the mice.

'Nice hat,' said Howard. 'I woke up and found you gone. What are you doing? What's going on?'

'We need you to carry all this,' said Mickey Thompson, waving a hand at the pile of stuff. 'We're going to fix the plane with it.'

'There's an apple core,' said Howard.

'Yes, Bangy de Gamba says—'

'OFF WE GO,' said Howard, quickly scooping everything

into a shopping basket and
leading the way through the
airport, past all the mess, under
the bridge, up the stairs, through
the room, down the ramp, into
the tunnel and back outside onto

the **wind y** runway
where Drummond was patiently
waiting.

'You came back!' he said, sounding relieved.

'Of course we did,' said Purvis. He opened "*Advanced Aerodynamics*" and turned to chapter 34.

'First,' he said, 'wrap Drummond's nose cone in Allen's aeroplane wrapping paper,' so they wrapped it.

'Now stick this on the end,' he said, handing over the football, so they stuck it.

'Whad id id?' said

Drummond, sounding all bunged up.

'That,' said Purvis, loosening it slightly, 'is a *High-performance Proboscis Protector*, to protect you from bumps and grazes.'

'*Ooh,*' said Drummond. 'That sounds impressive.'

'I know!' said Purvis. He turned over the page. 'Next, attach the *Rapid Deployment Drag Chute* to Drummond's tail.'

'The rapid de-whatty what what?' said Mickey Thompson.

'Here,' said Purvis, handing over the smart umbrella and the ball of string.

'Are we expecting rain?' asked Drummond.

'No,' said Purvis. 'It's to help with your landings: when the button's pressed, the umbrella will open and glide you down gently and these,' he said, rattling the tin of travel sweets, 'will stop queasiness.'

'Thank you,' said Drummond.

'I'm feeling queasy,' said

Mickey Thompson.

'They're for Drummond,' said Purvis.

'Oh, oh,' said Mickey Thompson, lying down and clutching his tummy.

'Let's all have one, to be on the safe side,' said Drummond, quickly, so they all did.

'And now I think we're ready,' said Purvis, once they'd eaten their sweets.

'Wait,' said Mickey Thompson.

'What?' said Purvis.

'I want to spray something gold.'

'Why?' said Purvis.

'So everything's *lovely* for Bangy de Gamba. How about the football?'

'Football?' said Drummond.

'*It isn't a football,*' whispered Purvis. '*It's a Proboscis Protector.*'

'It looks like a football,' said Mickey Thompson.

'I don't want to wear a football,' said Drummond. 'I

200

want to look my best for Bangy de Gamba.'

'Not you as well,' groaned Purvis, and Mickey Thompson brandished his can.

'Oh, go on, then,' said Purvis, so they sprayed the football burnished gold and looped the fairy lights around and around as a finishing touch.

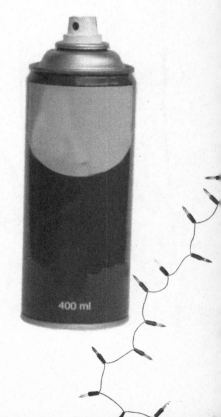

'Drummond looks

*lovely*,'

**sighed** Allen, and everyone
agreed that Drummond did.

'And now,' said Howard, 'I think we could all do with a cup of tea,' and everyone agreed that they could.

'Oh, could you, indeed,' said a familiar voice, and the mice and Allen dived under

Drummond just in time as Mr
Bullerton appeared and grabbed
hold of Howard's arm.

'Gotcha,' he said.

'Me too,' said the security
guard, running up and grabbing
hold of Howard's other arm.
'I'm handing you in to the
airport authorities.'

'Why?' said Howard.

'For not fixing the plane,
and for kicking the hat, and for
claiming your dog's a star when
he obviously isn't.'

'But, but,' *spluttered* Howard. 'I have, and I didn't, and my dog most certainly is a star, thank you very much.'

'Nonsense,' said Mr
Bullerton. 'You and your dog
are done for this time.'

'Yikes,' said Purvis.

'Oh dear, said Allen.

'BANGY!' said Mickey
Thompson, as there was a
sudden **kerfu*ff*le** on the
runway and Bangy de Gamba's
ride-on electric cart *whizzed*
up piled high with Bangy and
Ortrud and the heavies and
the driver and the pilot. They
*skidded* to a **halt** and all

climbed off.

'Oh boy,' said Bangy. 'This plane looks great! I love his golden schnoz.'

Drummond made a **gurgling** noise and Bangy waved at Mickey Thompson.

'Hi, Michael!' she said. 'Is that a new hat? It really suits you.'

Mickey Thompson made a **gurgling** noise as Mr Bullerton and the security guard stared at Bangy, open-mouthed.

'And you must be Howard,

and Allen,' said Bangy, going
over to them. 'Michael's told
me so much about you.' She
gave Howard a kiss on the cheek
and patted Allen's head, and
they both gurgled too.

'Your little elephant's been taking care of me,' Bangy told Howard.

'Elephant?' sniggered Mr Bullerton. 'What elephant?'

'The one I'm about to take on holiday,' said Bangy, winking at Ortrud. 'With all her friends, of course.'

Mr Bullerton made a *spluttering* noise.

'You can't,' said the security guard.

'Try and stop me,' said Bangy,

and she bustled Howard and Allen and Ortrud and the mice up Drummond's steps.

# 'COME BACK HERE,'

**roared** Mr Bullerton,

lunging at Howard and hanging onto his ankle.

'Hoy,' said Bangy

'Help,' said Howard.

'The doughnuts!' said Purvis. 'Quick!'

He shot down the steps, grabbed the box of **squashed** doughnuts Mickey Thompson had found and shot back up with it. Bangy took one and flung it, and everyone else flung some too.

'Take that!' *yelled* Bangy,

as the security guard and Mr Bullerton ran away, covered in custard.

'Purvis,' said Bangy, 'you are one clever cookie.'

Purvis made a **gurgling** noise and went a bright and very pleased pink.

'And now it's time we were going,' said Bangy, so they all climbed into Drummond and settled down comfortably.

Ready?' said Howard.

'Ready!' said the mice.

'Then let's fly out of here, fast,' said Howard…

And they did.

BY SORREL
ANDERSON
Clumsies

# The Clumsies

## make a mess

Illustrated by
nicola Slater

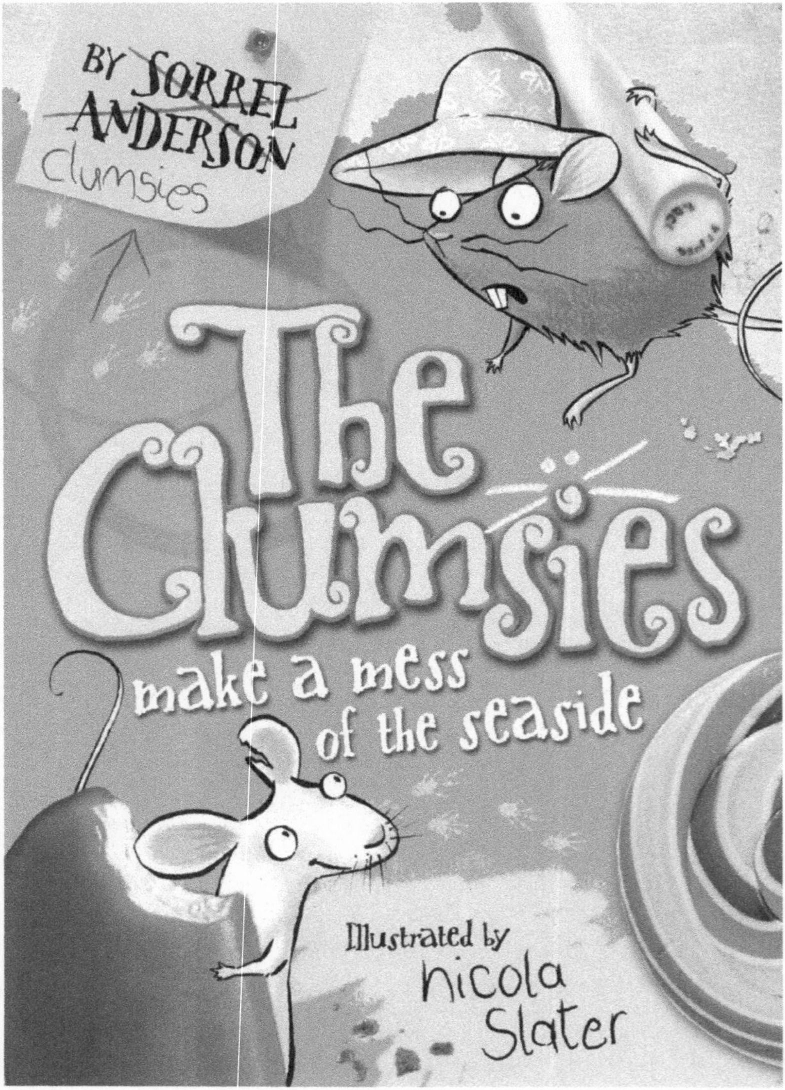

BY SORREL
ANDERSON
clumsies

# The Clumsies

make a mess
of the seaside

Illustrated by
nicola
Slater

BY SORREL ANDERSON

The Clumsies

make a mess of the BIG show

Illustrated by nicola Slater

SHORTLISTED FOR THE
The Roald Dahl FUNNY PRIZE

BY SORREL
ANDERSON

813072

The
Clumsies

make a
mess of the zoo

Illustrated by
nicola Slater

BY SORREL ANDERSON

# The Clumsies

## make a mess of the School

Illustrated by nicola Slater